The Jungle Book

Rudyard Kipling

Condensed and Adapted by
W.T. ROBINSON
KATHRYN R. KNIGHT

Illustrated by
RUTH PALMER

Cover Illustrated by
RUTH PALMER

Dalmatian Press

The Junior Classics have been
adapted and illustrated with care and thought
to introduce you to a world of famous authors, characters, ideas,
and great stories that have been loved for generations.

Editor — Kathryn Knight
Creative Director — Gina Rhodes Haynes
And the entire classics project team
of Dalmatian Publishing Group

THE JUNGLE BOOK

CE14742/0212 CLI

A note to the reader—

Three classic stories rest in your hands. The characters are famous. The tales are timeless.

This Junior Classic edition of well-known stories from *The Jungle Book* has been carefully condensed and adapted from the original versions (which you really *must* read when you're ready for every detail). We kept the well-known phrases for you. We kept Rudyard Kipling's style. And we kept the important imagery and heart of each tale.

Literature is terrific fun! It encourages you to think. It helps you dream. It is full of heroes and villains, suspense and humor, adventure and wonder, and new ideas. It introduces you to writers who reach out across time to say: "Do you want to hear a story I wrote?"

Curl up and enjoy.

ABOUT THE AUTHOR

RUDYARD KIPLING

Rudyard Kipling was born in Bombay (now Mumbai), India, on December 30, 1865. His parents were English, and he was sent to school in England at age six. He was not happy to be away at school, but he enjoyed writing. He published his first book, *Schoolboy Lyrics*, when he was sixteen.

In 1882 Kipling went to live with his parents in Pakistan. He became well known for his writings about the lives of soldiers. In 1889 he returned to England after traveling through Burma, China, Japan, and the United States.

After marrying an American, Kipling moved to Vermont. While there, he wrote *The Jungle Book* (1894) and *The Second Jungle Book* (1895), two of his most famous books.

Kipling enjoyed traveling, but he eventually settled in England. He wrote many books, including *Captains Courageous* (1897), *Kim* (1901), and *Just So Stories* (1902). In 1907 he became the first Englishman to win the Nobel Prize for Literature.

Kipling died in 1936 and is buried in Poet's Corner of Westminster Abbey.

CONTENTS

THE MOWGLI STORIES 1

1. The Man-Cub 3
2. The Wolf Pack Council 13
3. The Law of the Jungle 19
4. The *Bandar-log* 29
5. The Cold Lairs 41
6. Kaa's Hunting 49
7. Bagheera's Warning 59
8. The Red Flower 67
9. The Village 79
10. The Gathering 87
11. Tiger! Tiger! 97
12. The Return to Council Rock 107

THE WHITE SEAL 117

1. Kotick 119
2. "It's Horrible" 131
3. The Island 141

RIKKI-TIKKI-TAVI 157

1. Rikki-tikki Finds a Home 159
2. Rikki-tikki the Brave 177

This is the hour of pride and power,

Talon and tusk and claw.

Oh, hear the call!—Good hunting, all

That keep the Jungle Law!

—*Night-Song in the Jungle*

The Mowgli
Stories

MOWGLI — the man-cub adopted by wolves in the Jungle of India

WOLVES — the Wolf Pack that raises Mowgli
    MOTHER (RAKSHA) and FATHER WOLF
    AKELA (THE LONE WOLF) – wolf leader
    GREY BROTHER – Mowgli's wolf-brother

TABAQUI — the jackal

SHERE KHAN — the lame tiger

BALOO — the big brown bear who teaches Mowgli the Law of the Jungle

BAGHEERA — the black panther who helps to guide and protect Mowgli

BANDAR-LOG — the silly Monkey People

KAA — the thirty-foot rock python

CHIL — the kite (sea eagle)

VILLAGERS
    MESSUA – woman who takes Mowgli in
    BULDEO – hunter and old storyteller

RAMA — the big bull buffalo

CHAPTER ONE

The Man-Cub

It was seven o'clock on a very warm evening in the Seeonee hills. Father Wolf woke up, scratched himself, yawned, and spread out his paws. Mother Wolf lay with her big gray nose on her four tumbling, squealing cubs. The moon shone into the mouth of the cave.

"Augrh!" said Father Wolf. "It is time to hunt again."

Suddenly someone with a bushy tail called into the cave, "Good luck go with you, O Chief of the Wolves." It was the jackal—Tabaqui. The wolves of India hated Tabaqui. He made trouble. He told lies. He was often prowling for food scraps.

"There is no food here," said Father Wolf stiffly.

"For a wolf, no," said Tabaqui, "but for me, a dry bone is a good feast." He scuttled to the back of the cave, where he found a bone. "All thanks for this good meal," he said, licking his lips. "How beautiful are your noble children! How large are their eyes! Ah, little ones, beware! Shere Khan, the Big One, will hunt among these hills for the next moon, so he has told me."

Shere Khan was the lame tiger who lived near the Waingunga River, twenty miles away.

"He has no right!" Father Wolf began angrily. "By the Law of the Jungle he has no right to change his hunting grounds with no warning. He will frighten all our game within ten miles. Out!" he snapped. "Out and hunt with your master!"

"I go," said Tabaqui quietly. "Ah! You can hear Shere Khan below in the bushes."

Father Wolf listened. Below in the valley he heard the angry, snarly whine of a hungry tiger.

"The fool!" said Father Wolf. "To begin a night's work with that noise! Does he think that our bucks will not hear him?"

"H'sh. It is not buck he hunts tonight," said Mother Wolf. "It is Man."

"Man!" said Father Wolf, showing all his white teeth. "Are there not enough beetles and frogs in the ponds? Must he eat Man, and on our hunting ground, too?"

The Law of the Jungle never orders anything without a reason. And the Law forbids every beast to eat Man except when he is showing his children how to kill. Even then, he must hunt outside the hunting grounds of his pack or tribe. For man-killing means, sooner or later, that men will come with torches, and men on elephants with guns. Then everybody in the Jungle suffers.

The angry purr of the tiger grew loud and ended with the "Aaarh!" of the tiger's charge.

Then there was a howl—an un-tigerish howl—from Shere Khan.

"He has missed his kill," said Mother Wolf. "What is it?"

Father Wolf ran out a few steps and heard Shere Khan muttering as he tumbled about.

"The fool has jumped at a woodcutter's campfire and has burned his feet," said Father Wolf with a grunt. "Tabaqui is with him."

"Something is coming uphill," said Mother Wolf, twitching one ear. "Get ready."

The bushes rustled a little. Father Wolf got ready to leap. Then, if you had been watching, you would have seen the most wonderful thing in the world. Just as the wolf was leaping, he saw what it was he was jumping at, and then he tried to stop himself. He shot up straight into the air for four or five feet, landing almost where he left ground.

"Man!" he snapped. "A man's cub. Look!"

In front of him, holding on by a low branch, stood a naked brown baby who could just walk. He looked up into Father Wolf's face and laughed.

"Is that a man's cub?" said Mother Wolf. "I have never seen one. Bring it here."

Father Wolf's jaws closed on the child's back, but not a tooth even scratched the skin as he laid it down among the cubs.

"How little! And—how bold!" said Mother Wolf softly.

The baby pushed his way between the cubs to get close to the mother to nurse.

"*Ahai!* Now, was there ever a wolf that could say she had a man's cub among her children?"

"I have heard now and again of such a thing, but never in our Pack or in my time," said Father Wolf. "See how he looks up and is not afraid."

The moonlight was suddenly blocked out of the mouth of the cave by Shere Khan's great square head and shoulders. Tabaqui, behind him, was squeaking, "My lord, my lord, it went in here!"

"Shere Khan, you do us great honor," said Father Wolf, but his eyes were very angry. "What does Shere Khan need?"

"A man's cub went this way," said Shere Khan. "Its parents have run off. Give it to me."

Father Wolf knew that the mouth of the cave was too narrow for the tiger. "The Wolves are Free People," he said. "They take orders from the Head of the Pack, and not from any striped cattle-killer. The man-cub is ours."

"It is I, Shere Khan, who speak!" The tiger's roar filled the cave with thunder.

Mother Wolf shook herself clear of the cubs. She sprang forward, her eyes like two green moons in the darkness. She faced the blazing eyes of Shere Khan.

"And it is I, Raksha, the Demon, who answers. The man-cub is mine! He shall not be killed. He shall live to run with the Pack and to hunt with the Pack. And in the end he shall hunt *you*! Now, go!"

Father Wolf looked on amazed. Shere Khan might have faced Father Wolf, but he could not stand up against a mother wolf with cubs. So the tiger backed out of the cave growling. When he was clear he shouted:

"You may bark in your own yard. But we will see what the Pack will say to the raising of man-cubs. The cub is mine, and to my teeth he will come in the end!"

CHAPTER TWO

The Wolf Pack Council

Father Wolf turned to Mother Wolf. "Shere Khan speaks this much truth. The cub must be shown to the Pack. Will you still keep him, Mother?"

"Yes, I will keep him. Lie still, little frog. I will call you Mowgli, which means frog. Oh, little Mowgli, the time will come when you will hunt Shere Khan as he has hunted you."

"But what will our Pack say?" said Father Wolf.

The Law of the Jungle states that as soon as cubs are old enough to stand on their feet, they must be brought before the Pack Council so that all the wolves will then know them. Father Wolf waited till his cubs could run a little. On the night of the Pack Meeting he took them and Mowgli and Mother Wolf to Council Rock—a hilltop covered with stones where a hundred wolves could hide. Akela, the great gray Lone Wolf who led all the Pack, lay on his rock. Below him sat forty or more wolves of every size and color. There was very little talking at the Rock. The cubs tumbled over each other in the center of the circle while senior wolves looked at them carefully.

From his rock Akela cried, "Look well, O Wolves!"

Father Wolf pushed "Mowgli the Frog" into the center, where he sat laughing and playing with some pebbles.

"Look well!" Akela cried.

A muffled roar came up from behind the rocks—the voice of Shere Khan! "The cub is mine. Give him to me."

Akela never even twitched his ears. All he said was, "Look well, O Wolves!"

Now, the Law of the Jungle states that if there is any disagreement about a cub, at least two members of the Pack, other than his mother and father, must speak for him.

"Who of the Free People speaks for this cub?" said Akela.

There was no answer. Mother Wolf got ready to fight for her cub.

But there was one other creature allowed at the Pack Council—Baloo, the sleepy brown bear who teaches the wolf cubs the Law of the Jungle. Old Baloo could come and go where he pleased because he ate only nuts and roots and honey. Baloo rose up and grunted.

"The man's cub?" he said. "I speak for the man's cub. There is no harm in a man's cub. Let him run with the Pack. I myself will teach him."

"We need yet another," said Akela. "Baloo has spoken, and he is our teacher for the young cubs. Who speaks besides Baloo?"

A black shadow dropped down into the circle. It was Bagheera the black panther. Everybody knew Bagheera. He was cunning and bold, but he had a voice as soft as wild honey dripping from a tree.

"O Akela," he purred, "I know I have no right to speak here. But the Law of the Jungle says that the life of a cub may be bought at a price. And the Law does not say who may or may not pay that price. Am I right?"

"Speak, then," cried twenty voices.

"I will pay one bull, and a fat one, if you will accept the man's cub into the Pack."

There was a cry of voices. "Where is the bull, Bagheera? Let him be accepted."

And then came Akela's deep voice. "Look well—look well, O Wolves!"

Mowgli was still playing with the pebbles. He did not notice when the wolves came and looked at him one by one. Shere Khan roared in the night, for he was very angry that Mowgli had not been handed over to him.

"Yes, roar well," said Bagheera, under his whiskers, "for the time will come when this little thing will make you roar to another tune."

"It was well done," said Akela. "Men and their cubs are very wise. He may be a help in time." He turned to Father Wolf. "Take him away and train him."

And that is how Mowgli became part of the Seeonee Wolf Pack—for the price of a bull and on Baloo's good word.

CHAPTER THREE

The Law of the Jungle

Now you must skip five or six years, and only guess at the wonderful life that Mowgli led among the wolves. (If it were written out it would fill ever so many books.) He grew up with the cubs, and Father Wolf taught him the meaning of all things in the Jungle. Every rustle in the grass. Every breath of the warm night air. Every note of the owls. Every splash of every little fish jumping in a pool.

When he was not learning, he sat out in the sun and slept, and ate, and went to sleep again. When he felt dirty or hot, he swam in the forest pools. Baloo told him about honey and nuts. Bagheera showed

him how to climb for them. Bagheera would lie out on a branch and call, "Come along, Little Brother." He learned to fling himself through the branches almost as boldly as the gray ape. He played with his brothers and would pick out the long thorns that got into their pads.

These were the days when Baloo was teaching him the Law of the Jungle. The big, old brown bear was happy to have such a quick student. All young wolves learned about having "feet that make no noise, eyes that see in the dark, ears that hear the winds, and sharp white teeth." But Mowgli, as a man-cub, had to learn more than this.

Sometimes Bagheera came to see how the man-cub was doing, resting his head against a tree. The boy could climb almost as well as he could swim. He could swim almost as well as he could run. So Baloo, the Teacher of the Law, taught him the Wood and Water Laws:

How to tell a rotten branch from a good one.

How to speak politely to wild bees at the hive.

What to say if he has disturbed Mang the Bat during the day.

How to warn the water snakes before he splashed down in a pool.

Mowgli had to learn *all* the Law of the Jungle. He grew tired of saying the same thing over a hundred times. Sometimes Baloo gave the boy a gentle swat when he was not paying attention.

"Think how small he is," said Bagheera to Baloo one day. "How can his little head carry all your long talk?"

"Small things can be killed in the Jungle. That is why I teach him, and that is why I swat him, very softly, when he forgets."

"Softly! What do *you* know of softness, old Iron-feet?" Bagheera grunted.

"It is better for him to be punished by someone who loves him," said Baloo. "I am now teaching him the Master Words of the Jungle. They will protect him with the birds and the Snake People. I will call Mowgli and he will say them. Come, Little Brother!"

"My head is ringing like a bee tree," said a little voice over their heads. Mowgli slid down a tree trunk with an angry face. "I come for Bagheera—not for *you*, fat old Baloo!"

"That is fine with me," said Baloo, though he was a bit hurt. "Tell Bagheera, then, the Master Words of the Jungle I have taught you this day."

Mowgli was delighted to show off. "The Jungle has many tongues. *I* know them all." With a bear's growl, he gave the words of the Hunting People: "We be of one blood, you and I." With a whistle, he gave the words of the birds. With a hssss, he gave the words of the Snake People.

Baloo patted his big furry belly with pride. "He does not need to fear anyone," he said. "He is now safe in the Jungle, because neither snake, bird, nor beast will hurt him."

"Except his own tribe," said Bagheera quietly.

Mowgli danced about and pulled Bagheera's fur. "And so I shall have a tribe of my own!" he shouted. "And I shall lead them through the branches all day long."

"What is this foolishness, little dreamer of dreams?" said Bagheera.

"Yes, and I shall throw branches and dirt at old Baloo," Mowgli went on. "*They* have promised me this!"

"They?" said Baloo angrily. "*Whoof!*" The bear's big paw scooped Mowgli up. "Mowgli," he said, "you have been talking with the *Bandar-log*—the Monkey People—the people without a Law. That is great shame."

"When Baloo hurt my head," said Mowgli, "I went away, and the monkeys came down from the trees and felt sorry for me. No one else cared." He snuffled a little. "And they gave me nuts to eat. They carried me up to the top of the trees and said I was their blood-brother (except that I had no tail), and would be their leader someday."

"Bah! The Monkey People!" said Bagheera. "They lie. They have always lied."

"Listen, man-cub," said Baloo, with a voice like thunder. "We of the Jungle do not have anything to do with the Monkey People. We do not drink where the monkeys drink. We do not go where they go. We do not hunt where they hunt. They are foolish. They throw nuts and dirt on us—"

Just then, a shower of nuts and twigs rained down from the trees. They heard hoots and hollers above them.

"You must stay away from the Monkey People," Baloo growled.

The bear, the panther, and Mowgli trotted away as the monkeys hooted and threw nuts after them.

The Monkey People were upset. They had been so happy when Mowgli had come to play with them. (And now they heard how angry Baloo was!) They had decided that Mowgli would be a useful person to keep in the tribe. After all, he could weave sticks together. He could make little huts! Yes—he must join their tribe! Then they would have a leader and become the wisest people in the Jungle. And so, the monkeys followed Baloo and Bagheera and Mowgli through the Jungle very quietly till it was time for the midday nap.

CHAPTER FOUR

The *Bandar-log*

Mowgli was sleeping between the panther and the bear. Suddenly he felt hands on his legs and arms—hard, strong, little hands. Then he felt branches in his face. Then he was looking down from a tree! Baloo woke the Jungle with his deep cries. Bagheera scrambled up the trunk, showing his teeth. The *Bandar-log* howled and laughed and scuffled away to the upper branches where Bagheera would not dare to follow. The monkeys cheered, "Ha-ha! All the Jungle People admire us for our skill and cleverness." Then they hurried away through the treetops, taking Mowgli with them.

For a time Mowgli was afraid of being dropped. Then he grew angry and he began to plan. He knew his friends would be left far behind. Far away in the blue sky he saw Chil the kite.

"We be of one blood, you and I," called Mowgli to Chil. "Mark my trail! Tell Baloo of the Seeonee Pack and Bagheera of the Council Rock."

"In whose name, Brother?" Chil had never seen Mowgli before, though he had heard of him.

"Mowgli the Frog. Man-cub they call me! Mark my trail!"

Chil nodded and rose up till he looked no bigger than a speck of dust.

Meanwhile, Baloo and Bagheera were very upset and angry.

"Why did you not warn the man-cub?" Bagheera roared to poor Baloo as they ran through the Jungle.

"Hurry! Oh, hurry! We—we may catch them yet!" Baloo panted.

"This is no time for chasing. They may drop him if we follow too close," said the panther.

"*Arru-u-u-la!* They may have dropped him already!" moaned Baloo. "Oh, I am most miserable of bears! *Arulala!* Oh, Mowgli, Mowgli! Why did I not warn you more about the Monkey Folk?"

"Oh, do stop howling," said Bagheera. "At least he knows the Master Words of the Jungle," said Bagheera. "I have no fear for the man-cub. He is wise and well taught. And he has the eyes that make the Jungle People afraid. However, the *Bandar-log* have no fear of any of our people."

"Fool that I am!" said Baloo suddenly. "Oh, fat, brown, root-digging fool! The *Bandar-log* do fear one. They fear Kaa the rock python! He can climb as well as they can. He steals the young monkeys in the night. The whisper of his name makes their wicked tails cold. Let us go to Kaa."

"What will he do for us? He is not of our tribe—and he has evil eyes," said Bagheera.

"He is very old and very clever. And he is always hungry," said Baloo. "We will promise him many goats."

And they went off to look for Kaa. They found him stretched out in the afternoon sun. He had just spent ten days changing his skin, and now his thirty-foot self was very splendid.

"He has not eaten," said Baloo. "See—he is licking his lips. Be careful, Bagheera! He is always a little blind after he has changed his skin, and very quick to strike."

Kaa was not a poison snake. His strength lay in his hug. When he wrapped his huge coils around anybody, there was no more to be said.

"Good hunting!" cried Baloo.

Kaa did not hear well. He curled up and lowered his head.

"Good hunting for us all," he answered. "Oho, Baloo, what brings you here? Good hunting, Bagheera. Is there any news of game? A doe, or even a young buck? I am as empty as a dried well."

"We are hunting," said Baloo slowly. He knew that you must not hurry Kaa. He is too big.

"Allow me to come with you," said Kaa. "It has become too difficult for me to hunt in the trees. I came very near to falling on my last hunt—very near indeed. I slipped and waked the *Bandar-log*, and they called me most evil names."

"Yellow earthworm," mumbled Bagheera.

"*Sssss!* Have they called me *that*?" said Kaa.

"Yes—and they say that you have lost all your teeth," Bagheera said sweetly.

Kaa was angry. "When I came up into the sun today, I heard them whooping in the treetops."

"It—it is the *Bandar-log* that we follow now," admitted Baloo.

"The trouble is this, Kaa," said Bagheera: "Those nut-stealers and pickers of palm leaves have stolen away our man-cub."

"The best and wisest and boldest of man-cubs—my own pupil," said Baloo. "He shall make the name of Baloo famous through all the jungles. And besides, I—we—love him, Kaa."

"Our man-cub is in the hands of the *Bandar-log* now. We know that of all the Jungle People they only fear Kaa."

"They have good reason," said Kaa. "Foolish, chattering monkeys! They called me also—'yellow fish,' was it not?"

"Worm—worm—earthworm," said Bagheera, "as well as other things."

"*Aaa-ssp!*" snapped Kaa. "Now, where did they go with the cub?"

"The Jungle alone knows. Toward the sunset, I believe," said Baloo. "We had thought that you would know, Kaa."

"I? How? I take them when they come in my way, but I do not hunt the *Bandar-log*, or frogs—or green scum on a waterhole. *Hsss!*"

"Up, Up! Up, Up! Hello-ello-ello! Look up, Baloo of the Seeonee Wolf Pack!"

Baloo looked up. There was Chil, swooping down from the sky. It was near Chil's bedtime, but he had flown all over the Jungle looking for the bear.

"What is it?" said Baloo.

"I have seen Mowgli with the *Bandar-log*. He asked me tell you. I watched. The *Bandar-log* have taken him beyond the river to the Cold Lairs. I have told the bats to watch them. That is my message. Good hunting, all you below!"

"Good hunting—and many thanks to you, Chil," cried Bagheera.

"It is nothing. The boy knew the Master Word," called Chil as he flew off.

Baloo was filled with pride. "To think of one so young remembering the Master Word for the birds—while he was being pulled across trees!"

"He was taught well," said Bagheera. "I am proud of him. And now we must go to the Cold Lairs."

They all knew where that place was. Few of the Jungle People ever went there. It was an old city, now in ruins, deep in the Jungle.

"It is half a night's journey—at full speed," said Bagheera.

"I will go as fast as I can," said Baloo.

"We cannot wait for you," said Bagheera. "We must go on the quickfoot—Kaa and I. Baloo, you will follow."

"Feet or no feet, I can keep up with you," said Kaa. And they took off.

Baloo tried to hurry, but had to sit down panting. And so they left him to come on later.

Indeed the huge python went swiftly! No matter how Bagheera bounded, Kaa was right with him.

"You are no slow goer," said Bagheera to Kaa.

"I am hungry," said Kaa. "Besides, they called me a speckled frog."

"It was worm—earthworm."

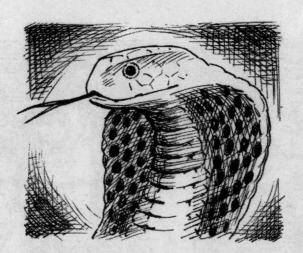

CHAPTER FIVE

The Cold Lairs

In the Cold Lairs the Monkey People were not thinking of Mowgli's friends at all. They were busy being very pleased with themselves.

Mowgli had never seen a city before. It was in ruins, but it seemed very wonderful and splendid. Some king had built it long ago. Trees and vines now grew between the walls and windows. On the top of the hill stood a great palace with no roof.

The monkeys called the place their city. They ran in and out of the temples and houses. They sat in the king's palace and scratched for fleas. They explored the dark hallways and tunnels. They told each other that they were doing what men do.

They gathered and shouted, "There is no one in the Jungle so wise and good and clever and strong and gentle as the *Bandar-log*!"

The monkeys dragged Mowgli into the old city late in the afternoon. They joined hands and danced about and sang their foolish songs. One of the monkeys announced that Mowgli was going to show them how to weave sticks to make a hut. Mowgli picked up some vines to weave. The monkeys watched for a few minutes, but then scampered away to play.

"I wish to eat," said Mowgli after a while.

Twenty or thirty monkeys ran off to bring him nuts, but they began to fight and ended up with nothing. Mowgli was angry as well as hungry.

"All that Baloo has said about the *Bandar-log* is true," he said to himself. "They have no Law and no leaders—nothing but foolish words and hands that steal. I must return to my own Jungle."

Mowgli walked to the city wall—but the monkeys pulled him back! They pinched him and told him he did not know how happy he was. Mowgli gritted his teeth and said nothing. But he laughed when they began to tell him how great and wise and strong and gentle they were.

"We are great. We are free. We are wonderful. We are the most wonderful people in all the Jungle! We all say so, and so it must be true!" they shouted.

The monkeys threw questions at Mowgli. Mowgli just nodded and blinked, and said "Yes." His head spun with the noise. "Do they never go to sleep? Now there is a cloud coming to cover that moon. I might try to run away in the darkness. But I am tired."

That same cloud was being watched by two good friends below the city wall. Bagheera and

Kaa were staying out of sight. They knew that the Monkey People were dangerous when they gathered in large numbers.

"I will go to the west wall," Kaa whispered. "I will come down swiftly. They will not throw themselves upon *my* back, but—"

"I know it," said Bagheera. "I wish that Baloo were here, but we must do what we can. They are having some sort of meeting with the boy over on that porch. When that cloud covers the moon I shall go there."

"Good hunting," said Kaa as he glided away.

The cloud now hid the moon. Mowgli wondered what would come next. Suddenly he heard Bagheera's light feet. The black panther had raced up and was striking right and left among the monkeys around Mowgli. There was a howl of fright and rage! A monkey shouted, "There is only one here! Kill him! Kill!" Monkeys began biting, scratching, tearing, and pulling at Bagheera.

Five or six monkeys grabbed Mowgli. They dragged him up a wall and pushed him through a hole. A boy trained by men would have been badly hurt, for the fall was a good fifteen feet. But Mowgli fell as Baloo had taught him to fall, and he landed on his feet.

"Stay there," shouted the monkeys, "till we have killed your friends. Later we will play with you—if the Poison People leave you alive."

Poison People! Mowgli knew they meant cobras—deadly snakes! He could hear hissing all around him. Mowgli quickly gave the Snake's Call.

"We be of one blood, you and I."

"Yessssss!" said many low voices. "Stand still, Little Brother, for your feet may do us harm."

Mowgli stood as quietly as he could. He could hear the yells and chatters of the monkeys fighting

Bagheera. For the first time since he was born, Bagheera was fighting for his life!

Baloo must be here. Bagheera would not have come alone, Mowgli thought. He called aloud, "To the water tank, Bagheera. Get to the water!"

Then came the rumbling war-shout of Baloo! "Bagheera," the bear shouted, "I am here! *Ahuwora!* The stones slip under my feet! But I am coming to battle the *Bandar-log*!"

He bounded onto the porch into a mob of monkeys. He spread out his forepaws and—*bat-bat-bat*—swatted at them.

Mowgli heard a crash and a splash. Ah! Bagheera had jumped into the water tank where the monkeys could not follow. The monkeys danced up and down with rage.

Bagheera lifted up his dripping chin and called Kaa with the Snake's Call.

"We be of one blood, you and I!"

CHAPTER SIX

Kaa's Hunting

Kaa had just worked his way over the west wall. He came quickly and ready to fight. A python four or five feet long can knock a man down if he hits him in the chest. Kaa was thirty feet long, as you know. He struck out at the surprised monkeys and knocked many down! The monkeys scattered with cries of—

"Kaa! It is Kaa! Run! Run!"

Kaa was everything that the monkeys feared in the Jungle. None of them could look him in the face. None had ever come alive out of his hug. And so they ran to the walls and the roofs of the houses, screaming in terror.

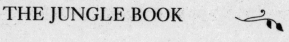

Then Kaa opened his mouth and spoke one long hissing word. The monkeys stopped their cries. Mowgli could hear Bagheera shaking his wet sides as he came up from the tank. Then the monkeys started leaping and screaming again.

"Get the man-cub out. I can do no more," Bagheera gasped. "Let us take the man-cub and go. They may attack again."

"They will not move till I order them. Ssstay!" Kaa hissed. The monkeys were silent once more.

"Baloo!" Bagheera called out. "Are you hurt?"

"It feels like they pulled me into a hundred little bearlings," said Baloo. He shook one leg after the other. "Wow! I am sore. Kaa, we owe you our lives."

"No matter," said the python. "Where is the manling?"

"Down here, in a trap! I cannot climb out!" cried Mowgli.

"Take him away," called the cobras. "He dances like a peacock. He will crush our young."

"Hah!" said Kaa with a chuckle. "He has friends everywhere, this manling. Stand back, manling. Go hide, Poison People. I will break down the wall."

Kaa found a crack in the wall. He lifted himself up and gave a great blow with his head, nose-first. The wall fell away in a cloud of dust! Mowgli leaped out and flung himself between Baloo and Bagheera—with an arm around each big neck.

"Are you hurt?" said Baloo, hugging him softly.

"I am sore, hungry, and a little hurt. But, my Brothers, how *you* are hurt! You bleed."

"Many monkeys bleed also," said Bagheera, licking his lips.

"It is nothing, it is nothing, if you are safe!" whimpered Baloo.

"We owe the battle and your life to Kaa," said Bagheera. "Thank him, Mowgli."

Mowgli turned. The great python's head swayed a foot above him.

"Sssso this is the manling," said Kaa. "Very soft is his skin. He looks like a monkey. Be careful, manling, that I do not mistake you for a monkey some night after I have just changed my coat."

"We be of one blood, you and I," Mowgli answered. "I owe you for my life tonight. I have some skill in these." He held out his hands. "If ever any of you are in a trap, I may free you. Good hunting to you all, my masters."

"Well said," growled Baloo. Mowgli had returned thanks very well.

"All thanks, Little Brother," said Kaa. His eyes twinkled. "You have a brave heart. This shall carry you far through the Jungle, manling. But now go quickly with your friends. Go and sleep, for the moon sets. You should not see what follows."

The moon was sinking behind the hills. Monkeys huddled together on the walls. Bagheera licked his fur. Baloo went down to the water tank for a drink. Kaa glided out into the center of the porch. *Snap!* went his jaws. All the monkeys' eyes were upon him.

"The moon setsss," he said. "Is there ssstill enough light to sssee?"

From the walls came a moan like the wind in the treetops. "We see, O Kaa."

"Good. Now begins the dance—the Dance of the Hunger of Kaa. Sit sssstill and watch."

He turned in big circles, weaving his head from right to left. He made loops and coils with his body, slowly, slowly, humming softly. The monkeys could not move. They were hypnotized.

Baloo and Bagheera stood still as stone. Mowgli watched and wondered.

"*Bandar-log,*" said the voice of Kaa at last. "Can you move without my order? Ssspeak!"

"We cannot, O Kaa!"

"Good! Come clossser to me."

The monkeys swayed and stepped forward in a trance. And Baloo and Bagheera took one step forward with them.

"Clossser!" hissed Kaa. They all moved again.

Mowgli laid his hands on Baloo and Bagheera to get them away. The two friends shook as if from a dream.

"Keep your hand on me," Bagheera whispered. "Keep it there, or I will go back—must go back to Kaa. *Aah!*"

"It is only old Kaa making circles on the dust," said Mowgli. "Let us go."

And the three slipped off to the Jungle.

"*Whoof!*" said Baloo. "Never more will I make a friend of Kaa." He shook himself all over.

"If I had stayed, I would have walked down his throat," added Bagheera with a tremble.

"Many will walk that way before the moon rises again," said Baloo. "He will have good hunting—in his own way."

Bagheera turned to Mowgli. His face was stern. "All this fighting tonight, man-cub, is because you played with the *Bandar-log*."

"It is true," said Mowgli sadly. "I am a bad man-cub. My belly is sad in me."

"*Hmm!* What does the Law of the Jungle say, Baloo?" asked the panther.

Baloo looked at Mowgli with big sad eyes. "The Law says that being sorry does not mean there is no punishment," he mumbled. "But remember, Bagheera, he is very little."

"I will remember. But he has done mischief. Mowgli, do you have anything to say?"

"Nothing. I did wrong. Baloo and you are wounded. It is right that I be punished."

Bagheera gave him a few love-taps. To a panther, these were soft taps. But not for a seven-year-old boy. When it was all over, Mowgli sneezed and picked himself up without a word.

"Now," said Bagheera, "jump on my back, Little Brother. We will go home."

In Jungle Law, punishment closes the matter. There is no nagging afterward.

Mowgli laid his head down on Bagheera's back and slept deeply. He did not even wake up when he was put down by Mother Wolf's side in the home-cave.

CHAPTER SEVEN

Bagheera's Warning

Now you must skip another five years. Mowgli kept at his lessons with Baloo. He learned to be crafty in the hunt. He loved his life in the Jungle.

What Mowgli loved best was to go with Bagheera into the dark warm heart of the forest, to sleep all through the drowsy day, and at night see how Bagheera did his hunting. And sometimes he would go down the hillside and peek at the villagers in their huts.

He grew tall and strong and brave. Mother Wolf told him once or twice that Shere Khan was not a creature to be trusted, and that someday he must kill Shere Khan.

Shere Khan was always crossing his path in the Jungle. He had become great friends with the younger wolves of the Pack, who followed him for scraps. Shere Khan teased them about their man-cub brother. "They tell me that you fear him," he said. "I hear that you dare not look him in the eyes." And the young wolves would growl.

Bagheera, who had eyes and ears everywhere, knew something of this. Once or twice he told Mowgli that Shere Khan would kill him someday. Mowgli would laugh and answer, "I have the Pack and I have you and Baloo, though he is so lazy. Why should I be afraid?"

One very warm day, deep in the Jungle, Mowgli lay with his head on Bagheera's beautiful black skin. "Little Brother," said the panther, "how often have I told you that Shere Khan is your enemy?"

"As many times as there are nuts on that palm," said Mowgli, who, of course, could not count. "What of it? I am sleepy, Bagheera, and Shere Khan is all long tail and loud talk—like Mao the peacock."

"But this is no time for sleeping. Baloo knows it. I know it. The Pack know it. Open those eyes, Little Brother. Shere Khan would dare not kill you in the Jungle. Remember, Akela is very old, and soon the day comes when he will be leader no more. Many of the wolves that raised you are old, too. But the young wolves believe, as Shere Khan has taught them, that a man-cub has no place with the Pack. In a little time you will be a man."

"I was born in the Jungle. I have obeyed the Law of the Jungle. The wolves are my brothers!"

Bagheera half shut his eyes. "Little Brother," said he, "feel under my jaw."

Mowgli put up his strong brown hand. Just under Bagheera's silky chin he felt a bald spot.

"No one in the Jungle knows that *I*, Bagheera, carry that mark—the mark of the collar. Yes, I too was born among men, in the cages of the King's Palace. I had never seen the Jungle. They fed me behind bars from an iron pan. Then, one night, I felt that I was Bagheera—the Panther—and no man's plaything. I broke the silly lock with one blow of my paw and ran away. And because I had learned the ways of men, I became more terrible in the Jungle than Shere Khan. Is it not so?"

"Yes," said Mowgli. "All in the Jungle fear Bagheera—all except Mowgli."

"You are a man's cub," said the black panther very tenderly. "And just as *I* returned to my Jungle, so *you* must go back to men at last—to the men who are your brothers—if you are not killed in the Council."

"But why—but why should any wish to kill me?" said Mowgli.

"The young ones hate you because they cannot look you in the eyes. They know you are wise—because you are a man-cub. And I know in my heart that when Akela is gone, the Pack will turn against you. They will hold a Jungle Council at the Rock, and then—and then. . . I have it!" said Bagheera, leaping up. "Go down quickly to the men's huts in the valley. Take some of the Red Flower they grow there. Then you will have even a stronger friend than I or Baloo or those of the Pack that love you. Get the Red Flower."

By Red Flower Bagheera meant fire, only no creature in the Jungle will call fire by its real name. Every beast lives in deadly fear of it.

"The Red Flower?" said Mowgli. "That grows outside their huts at night. I will get some."

"Spoken like a man's cub," said Bagheera proudly. "Remember that it grows in little pots. Get one swiftly, and keep it by you for time of need."

"Good!" said Mowgli. "I go. I go tonight." And he bounded away.

"That is a man. That is all a man," said Bagheera to himself. "Oh, Shere Khan, you never should have had that frog-hunt ten years ago!"

CHAPTER EIGHT

The Red Flower

That night, Mowgli plunged down through the bushes to the stream at the bottom of the valley. There he stopped. He heard the yell of the Pack hunting. He heard the snort of a buck and the howls of the young wolves. One wolf called:

"Akela! Akela! Room for the leader of the Pack! Spring, Akela!"

Mowgli heard the snap of Akela's teeth and then a yelp as the buck kicked him. Akela must have sprung and missed. Akela was too old to hunt and lead.

"Bagheera spoke truth," Mowgli said. "To-morrow Akela will be gone—and so will I."

He ran into the croplands where the villagers lived, and sat down near a hut. He pressed his face to a window and watched all night. A fire glowed in the fireplace. A woman got up to feed the fire with black lumps. When the misty morning came, a child picked up a pot, filled it with red-hot lumps, put it under his wrap, and went out to tend the cows.

"Is that all?" said Mowgli. "If a cub can do it, there is nothing to fear." So he rushed to the boy and took the pot from his hands. Then Mowgli ran off into the mist while the boy howled with fear.

"They are very like me," said Mowgli. He blew into the pot as he had seen the woman do. "This thing will die if I do not give it things to eat." He dropped twigs and dried bark on the red stuff. Halfway up the hill he met Bagheera.

"Akela has missed," said the panther. "They were looking for you on the hill."

"I am ready. See!" Mowgli held up the fire pot.

"Good! Now, I have seen men thrust a dry branch into that stuff. The Red Flower then bloomed at the end of it. Are you afraid?"

"No. Why should I fear? I remember now— from before I was a wolf—I would lie beside the Red Flower in a hut. It was warm and pleasant."

All that day Mowgli sat in the cave tending his fire pot and dipping dry branches into it to see how they looked. He found a branch he liked. Then Mowgli went to the Council that night. He was laughing.

Akela lay by the side of his rock. Shere Khan sat smugly with his troop of young wolves. Bagheera lay close to Mowgli, and the fire pot was between Mowgli's knees. Because there was now no leader, Shere Khan began to speak.

"He has no right," whispered Bagheera to Mowgli. "Say so. He will be frightened."

Mowgli sprang to his feet. "Free People," he cried, "does Shere Khan, a tiger, lead the Pack?"

Many wolves yelled out.

"Silence, man's cub!"

"Let him speak. He has kept our Law."

"Let Akela speak!"

Akela raised his old head. "Free People, for twelve seasons I have led you in the hunt. Now I have missed my kill. You have the right to kill me here on the Council Rock now. Therefore, I ask, who comes to make an end of me, the Lone Wolf?"

There was a long hush. No wolf cared to fight Akela to the death. Then Shere Khan roared—

"Bah! Why kill him? He will die soon, anyway. It is the man-cub who has lived too long. He was mine from the first. Give him to me. Give me the man-cub!"

Akela lifted his head again. "He has eaten our food. He has slept with us. He has hunted with us. He has broken no word of the Law of the Jungle."

"No man's cub can run with the People of the Jungle," howled Shere Khan. "Give him to me!"

"He is our brother," Akela went on, "and you would kill him here? In truth, I have lived too long. It is certain that I must die. My life is of no worth, or I would offer that in the man-cub's place. But, for the sake of the Honor of the Pack, I promise that if you let the man-cub go to his own place, I will not, when my time comes to die, bare one tooth against you. I will die without fighting."

"He is a man—a man—a man!" snarled the Pack. And most of the wolves began to gather around Shere Khan, whose tail was beginning to switch.

"Now," Bagheera said to Mowgli. "*We* can do no more except fight."

Mowgli stood up with the fire pot in his hands and his heart filled with rage and sorrow.

"Listen you!" he cried. "I would have been a wolf with you to my life's end. But I see now that you hate me. But you have told me so often tonight that I am a man, that I feel your words are true. So I do not call you my brothers anymore. I call you dogs! And I, the man, have brought here a little of the Red Flower which you dogs fear!"

He flung the fire pot on the ground. Some of the red coals lit some dried moss that flared up. The Council drew back in terror.

Mowgli thrust his dead branch into the fire till the twigs lit and crackled. He whirled it above his head among the frightened wolves.

"Good!" said Mowgli, looking around. "I see that you are dogs. I go from you to my own people—if they *are* my own people. The Jungle is shut to me, and I must forget you. But I will show mercy to you. I promise that when I am a man among men, I will not betray you to men as you have betrayed me." He kicked the fire with his foot and the sparks flew up. "But before I go . . ." He walked over to Shere Khan and grabbed the hair of his chin. "Up, dog!" Mowgli cried. "Up, when a man speaks, or I will set that coat ablaze!"

Shere Khan's ears lay flat back on his head. He shut his eyes, for the blazing branch was very near.

"This dog said he would kill me. Ha! This is how men beat dogs!" He beat Shere Khan over the head with the branch. The tiger whimpered in fear.

Mowgli now turned to the others. "When next I come to the Council Rock, as a man, it will be with Shere Khan's hide on my head. As for Akela, I command that he go free to live as he pleases. You will *not* kill him. Now, go!"

The fire blazed at the end of the branch. Mowgli struck right and left around the circle, and the wolves ran howling with the sparks burning their fur. At last there were only Akela, Bagheera, and ten wolves that had stayed loyal to Mowgli.

Something began to hurt Mowgli inside him. He had never hurt like this before in his life. He caught his breath and sobbed, and the tears ran down his face.

"What is it? What is it?" he said. "I do not wish to leave the Jungle, and I do not know what this is. Am I dying, Bagheera?"

"No, Little Brother. That is only tears such as men use," said Bagheera. "Now I know you are a man, no longer a man's cub. Let them fall, Mowgli. They are only tears."

So Mowgli sat and cried as though his heart would break.

"Now," said Mowgli, "I will go to men. But first I must say farewell to my mother."

He went to the cave where she lived with Father Wolf. He cried on her coat, while her four new cubs howled miserably.

"You will not forget me?" said Mowgli.

"Never," said the cubs. "Come to the foot of the hill when you are a man, and we will talk to you. We will come into the croplands to play with you by night."

"Come soon!" said Father Wolf. "Oh, wise little frog, come again soon, for we are old, your mother and I."

"Come soon," said Mother Wolf, "little son of mine, whom I loved more than I loved my cubs."

"I will surely come," said Mowgli, "and when I come, it will be to lay out Shere Khan's hide upon the Council Rock. Do not forget me! Tell them in the Jungle never to forget me!"

The dawn was beginning to break. Mowgli went down the hillside alone, to meet those mysterious things that are called men.

CHAPTER NINE

The Village

Mowgli went down to the plowed lands near the village. He would not stop there because it was too near to the Jungle. So he hurried on. He kept to the valley road for nearly twenty miles, till he came to a country that he did not know. On one side stood a little village, and at the other he could see the thick Jungle. He saw cattle and buffaloes being tended by boys. When the boys saw Mowgli they shouted and ran away. Mowgli was feeling hungry, and when he came to the village gate he saw that it was blocked with thorny branches.

"Umf!" he said, sitting down by the gate. "So men are afraid of the People of the Jungle here."

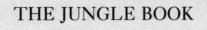

When a man came out, Mowgli stood up and opened his mouth to show that he wanted food. The man looked startled. He ran into the village and shouted for the priest. The priest, along with a hundred others, came to the gate. They stared and talked and shouted and pointed at Mowgli.

"They have no manners, these Men Folk," said Mowgli to himself. "Only the gray ape would behave as they do." So he threw back his long hair and frowned at the crowd.

"What is there to be afraid of?" said the priest. "Look at the marks on his arms and legs. They are the bites of wolves. He is a wolf-child who has run away from the Jungle."

"*Ah! Ah!*" said two or three women together. "Poor child! He is a handsome boy. He has eyes like red fire. Come see, Messua. He looks like your little boy who was taken by the tiger."

"Let me look," said a woman with big copper bracelets. She looked closely at Mowgli. "Indeed he is not. He is thinner, but he has the very look of my boy."

But the priest looked up at the sky for a minute and said, "What the Jungle has taken, the Jungle has given back. Take the boy into your house."

"Well," said Mowgli to himself, "if I am a man, a man I must become."

So the woman took Mowgli to her hut. She gave him a long drink of milk and some bread. Then she laid her hand on his head and looked into his eyes. "Nathoo? Are you my Nathoo who was taken by the tiger?" Mowgli did not reply. "Do you remember the day I gave you new shoes?" She touched his foot. "No," she said sadly, "those feet have never worn shoes. But you are very like my Nathoo, and you shall be my son."

Mowgli was uneasy. He had never been under a roof before. He felt foolish for he did not know man's talk. Mowgli had learned to sound just like the wolves, the birds, the wild pigs, and other animals in the Jungle. *I must learn man's talk*, he thought. So, when Messua said a word, Mowgli would try to make the same sound. Before dark he had learned the names of many things in the hut.

At bedtime, Mowgli could not sleep in a closed-in place. And when they shut the door he went through the window.

"Let him have his way," said Messua's husband. "Remember, he has never slept on a bed. He will not run away."

So Mowgli stretched himself in some long, clean grass near the field. Just as he was closing his eyes, a soft gray nose poked him under the chin.

"Ugh!" said Grey Brother. (This was the oldest of Mother Wolf's cubs.) "I have followed you twenty miles. Ugh—you smell like wood-smoke and cattle. You're like a man already. Wake up, Little Brother. I bring news."

Mowgli hugged him. "Is everyone well in the Jungle?"

"All except the wolves that were burned with the Red Flower. Now, listen. Shere Khan has gone away to hunt far off till his coat grows again, for he was badly burned. When he returns he swears that he will lay your bones in the river."

"I also have made a little promise," said Mowgli. "But I am tired tonight—very tired with new things, Grey Brother—but bring me the news always."

"You will not forget that you are a wolf, will you? Men will not make you forget?" said Grey Brother.

"Never. I will always remember that I love you and all in our cave. But also I will always remember that I have been cast out of the Pack."

"And you may be cast out of another pack," said the wolf, looking toward the village. "Men are only men, Little Brother. They talk like the frogs in a pond. When I come down here again, I will wait for you over in the bamboo."

CHAPTER TEN

The Gathering

For three months Mowgli was busy learning the ways of men. He had to wear clothes, which annoyed him. He learned about money (which he did not understand) and about farming and plowing. Sometimes the little children made him angry. They made fun of him when he would not play games or fly kites. They laughed when he said words the wrong way. Luckily the Law of the Jungle had taught Mowgli to keep his temper.

One day, the priest told Messua's husband that Mowgli would need to start working. He would go out with the buffaloes the next day and herd them while they grazed. This pleased Mowgli.

That night, he went to the gathering under a great fig tree, for now Mowgli felt a part of the village. At the gathering, people told gossip and sang songs. Monkeys sat and talked in the upper branches. A cobra, fed with a bowl of milk, was kept in a pit by the tree. The old men sat around and smoked pipes. They told wonderful tales of gods and men and ghosts. One old hunter, Buldeo, told even more wonderful tales of the ways of beasts in the Jungle. The eyes of the children grew wide as they listened. Most of the tales were about animals, for the Jungle was always at their door.

Deer and wild pigs grubbed up their crops. Now and again the tiger carried off a man in early evening, within sight of the village gates.

Mowgli, of course, knew much about the Jungle. He had to cover his face, for he chuckled at some of Buldeo's foolish stories. Buldeo told how the tiger that had carried away Messua's son was a ghost-tiger. "The tiger walks with a limp, so he must be the ghost of the wicked old man from the village who also had a limp."

"True, true. That must be the truth," said the old men, nodding.

"Are all these tales such cobwebs and moon talk?" said Mowgli. "That tiger limps because he was born lame. To say that a wicked man's soul is in a beast—that is child's talk."

Buldeo was speechless with surprise.

"Oho! It is the jungle brat, is it?" said Buldeo. "If you are so wise about this tiger, bring his hide to the city, for there is a reward on his life. Better still, talk not when your elders speak."

Mowgli rose to go. "All evening I have listened," he called back over his shoulder. "Except once or twice, Buldeo has not said one word of truth about the Jungle. So why should I believe his tales of ghosts and gods and goblins?"

Buldeo puffed and snorted at Mowgli's rude words, and one man said, "It is time that boy went to herding."

In the villages of India it is the boys who take the cattle and buffaloes out to graze in the early morning. Then they bring them back at night. The boys do not fear tigers. As long as the boys keep with the herds they are safe. Not even the tiger will charge a mob of cattle. But if a boy wanders off to pick flowers or hunt lizards, he is sometimes carried off.

Now it was Mowgli's time to herd. That morning, he went through the village street, sitting on the back of Rama, the great herd bull. The big, blue buffaloes, with their long, backward-sweeping horns and savage eyes, rose and followed him. Mowgli made it very clear to the other children that he was the master. He told Kamya, one of the boys, to graze the cattle by themselves. He, Mowgli, would tend to the buffaloes.

The grazing ground was rocky with scrubby plants and little streams. The buffaloes liked to keep to the pools where they could lie in the warm mud for hours. So Mowgli drove them on to where the Waingunga River came out of the Jungle. Then he dropped from Rama's neck and trotted off to a bamboo clump. There he found Grey Brother.

"Ah," said Grey Brother, "I have waited here many days. What is the meaning of this cattle-herding work?"

"It is an order," said Mowgli. "I am a village herd-boy for a while. What is the news of Shere Khan?"

"He came back and waited here a long time for you. Now he has gone off again. But he wants to kill you."

"Very good," said Mowgli. "As long as he is away, come sit on that rock, so that I can see you as I come out of the village. When he comes back, wait for me by the *dhâk* tree in the center of the grassy plain. We don't want to walk into Shere Khan's mouth."

Then Mowgli lay down in a shady place and slept while the buffaloes grazed around him. Herding in India is a lazy job. The cattle just move slowly, crunch, grunt, and lie down. The buffaloes get down into the muddy pools till only their noses and eyes show above the mud.

The young herders sleep and wake and sleep again. They weave little baskets of dried grass and put grasshoppers in them. They may catch two praying mantises and make them fight. They string a necklace of red and black jungle nuts. They look for lizards, snakes, and frogs. They sing long, long songs. Perhaps they make a mud castle with mud figures of men and horses and buffaloes.

When evening comes, the children call the cattle in, and the buffaloes lumber up out of the sticky mud. They all cross the grassy plain back to the twinkling village lights.

Day after day Mowgli would lead the buffaloes to the mud, and day after day he would see Grey Brother sitting on the rock across the plain. So he knew that Shere Khan had not come back. And day after day he would lie on the grass listening to the noises around him, and dreaming of old days in the Jungle.

At last a day came when he did not see Grey Brother on the rock. Mowgli laughed and headed the buffaloes for the *dhâk* tree, which was all covered with golden-red flowers.

There sat Grey Brother.

CHAPTER ELEVEN

Tiger! Tiger!

"He is back, hot on your trail," panted the wolf. Mowgli frowned. "I am not afraid of him."

"Shere Khan's plan is to wait for you at the village gate this evening—for you and for no one else. He is lying up now in the dry river gully."

"Has he eaten today, or does he hunt empty?" said Mowgli.

"He killed a pig at dawn, and he has drunk, too."

"Oh! Fool! Eaten and drunk, too! And he thinks that I shall wait till he has slept? Ha! Now, where is he? I can drive the buffaloes to charge him. But they will not charge unless they smell him, and I cannot speak their language."

"He swam far down the river through the valley. He lies at the bottom in the gully where the walls are steep," said Grey Brother.

Mowgli stood with his finger in his mouth, thinking. "The river valley. That opens out on the plain not half a mile from here. I can take the herd around through the Jungle to the top of the valley and then sweep down—but he would slink out at the bottom. We must block that end. Grey Brother, can you cut the herd in two for me?"

"Not I, perhaps—but I have brought a wise helper." Grey Brother trotted off and dropped into a hole. Then a huge gray head popped up that Mowgli knew well.

"Akela! Akela!" said Mowgli, clapping his hands. "You did not forget me! We have much work to do. Cut the herd in two, Akela. Keep the cows and calves together, and the bulls and the plow buffaloes by themselves."

The two wolves ran in and out of the herd. They herded the cow-buffaloes and their calves into the center. The cows glared and pawed the ground, ready to trample the wolves. The wolves herded the bulls and the young bulls into a separate clump. No six men could have divided the herd so neatly.

"What are your orders now?" panted Akela.

Mowgli slipped onto Rama's back. "Drive the bulls away, Akela, to the top of the valley. Grey Brother, when we are gone, drive the cows down into the bottom at the gully—then head up."

"How far up the gully?" said Grey Brother.

"Till the rocky walls are higher than Shere Khan can jump," shouted Mowgli. "Keep them there till we come down."

Akela howled and herded the bulls off to the left. Mowgli followed atop Rama.

Grey Brother stepped in front of the cows. They charged down on him, and he ran just before them, leading them down to the gully.

"Well done!" Mowgli said. "Now, turn, Akela! Swiftly turn them! Into the Jungle and to the top of the valley!"

Akela herded the bulls to the right, crashing through the thicket. The other herd-children saw this from far off. They hurried to the village as fast as their legs could carry them, crying, "The buffaloes have gone mad and run away!"

But Mowgli's plan was simple. All he wanted to do was make a big circle uphill and get at the top of the valley. Then he would take the bulls down it, while Grey Brother was charging the cows up from the bottom. In between would be Shere Khan—caught between the bulls and cows. Mowgli knew that after a meal and a full drink, Shere Khan would not be able to fight or claw up the sides of the gully. It was a long, long circle, for they did not wish to give Shere Khan warning.

At the top, Mowgli looked down into the river valley. *Good*, he thought. *The walls down below run nearly straight up and down. No tiger can climb those walls.*

"Let the buffaloes breathe, Akela," he said, holding up his hand. "I must tell Shere Khan who comes. We have him in the trap."

He put his hands to his mouth and shouted down the valley. It was almost like shouting down a tunnel. The echoes jumped from rock to rock.

After a long time, a sleepy, snarly voice cried, "Who calls?"

"I, Mowgli. It is time to come to the Council Rock, cattle-thief! Down—hurry them down, Akela! Down, Rama, down!"

Once the herd started, there was no chance of stopping. Halfway down the valley, they smelled the tiger. Rama bellowed!

"Ha! Ha!" said Mowgli. "Now you know!"

Rama and the buffaloes stampeded down the gully like boulders. Shere Khan heard the thunder of their hooves. He picked himself up and lumbered down the gully, looking from side to side for some way of escape. The rocky walls went straight up, so he had to keep moving ahead. But in front of him he heard more hooves, more snorting! He was heavy with his dinner and his drink. He did not want to fight. He had nowhere to turn.

Mowgli and the buffaloes were now almost atop the tiger. Mowgli saw Shere Khan turn to face them. Then Rama tripped, stumbled, and went on again over something soft. The bulls at his heels crashed into the other herd of cows. Both herds stamped and bellowed, kicked and roared. Horns locked with horns. The huge beasts tumbled over each other toward the bottom of the gully and spilled out into the open plain.

"Quick, Akela! Grey Brother!" called Mowgli. "Break them up. Scatter them, or they will be fighting one another. Drive them away, Akela. *Hai*, Rama! *Hai, hai, hai!* It is all over."

Shere Khan was dead, and the eagles were coming for him already.

Mowgli pulled out the knife he carried around his neck. "His hide will look well on the Council Rock. We must get to work swiftly."

CHAPTER TWELVE

The Return to Council Rock

Most boys could never skin a ten-foot tiger alone. It was hard work, but Mowgli knew how an animal's skin is fitted on, and how it is taken off.

After an hour, Mowgli felt a hand on his shoulder. It was Buldeo. The children had told the village about the buffalo stampede. Buldeo had come to punish Mowgli for not taking better care of the herd. The wolves dropped out of sight.

"What is this?" said Buldeo angrily. "You think you can skin a tiger? Where did the buffaloes kill him? It is the Lame Tiger, too, and there is a reward for his hide. Well, well, perhaps I will give you one silver coin when I have turned it in."

"Hm!" said Mowgli quietly. "So you will take the hide for the reward, and perhaps give me one coin? Now, it is in *my* mind that I need the skin for my *own* use. Heh!"

"How dare you talk this way to the chief hunter of the village, little beggar brat. I will not give you one bit of the reward, but only a very big beating. Leave the tiger!"

Mowgli went on skinning. "Akela," he called, "this man bothers me."

Buldeo soon found himself flat on the grass with a gray wolf standing over him.

"Ye–es," said Mowgli quietly. "You are right, Buldeo. You will never give me one bit of the reward. There is an old war between this lame tiger and myself—a very old war, and—I have won."

Buldeo whimpered. "This boy speaks to wolves!" he said. "This is magic! Bad magic!" He lay still, expecting every minute to see Mowgli turn into a tiger. "Great Magician," he whispered.

"Yes," chuckled Mowgli, not turning his head.

"I am an old man. I did not know that you were anything more than a herd-boy. May I rise up and go away, or will your servant tear me to pieces?"

"Go, and peace go with you. Let him go, Akela."

Buldeo hobbled away to the village as fast as he could. When he got there he told a tale of magic that made the priest look very grave.

Mowgli went on with his work. It was evening before he had finished skinning the tiger.

"Now we must take the buffaloes home. Help me herd them, Akela."

When they got near the village, Mowgli saw lights. Half the village seemed to be waiting for him by the gate. "That is because I have killed Shere Khan," he said to himself. But instead of happy shouts, Mowgli heard stones whistle about his ears. He heard cries of "Wolf's brat! Jungle demon! Go away, wolf!"

"What is this?" said Mowgli, as the stones flew thicker.

"They are like the Pack, these brothers of yours," said Akela, sitting down. "They, too, are casting you out."

"Again? Last time it was because I was a man. This time it is because I am a wolf. Let us go, Akela." He turned to the villagers. "Farewell, children of men," he called. "I will do your herding no more. Be thankful that I do not come in with my wolves and hunt you up and down your street."

He walked away with the Lone Wolf. As he looked up at the stars he felt happy. "No more sleeping in huts for me, Akela. Let us get Shere Khan's hide and go away. No, we will not hurt the village, for Messua was kind to me."

The moon was just going down when Mowgli and the two wolves came to the hill of the Council Rock. They stopped at Mother Wolf's cave.

"They have cast me out from the Man Pack, Mother," shouted Mowgli, "but I come with the hide of Shere Khan to keep my word."

Mother Wolf walked stiffly from the cave with her four cubs behind her. Her eyes glowed as she saw the skin. "I told him on that day, when he crammed his head and shoulders into this cave, hunting for your life, Little Frog—I told him that the hunter would be the hunted. It is well done."

"Little Brother, it is well done," said a deep voice in the thicket. "We were lonely in the Jungle without you." Bagheera came running to Mowgli's bare feet.

They went up to Council Rock together, and Mowgli spread the hide out on the flat stone where Akela used to sit. Akela lay down upon it, and called the old call to the Council.

"Look—look well, O Wolves," called Akela, exactly as he had called when Mowgli was first brought there.

Ever since Akela had been cast out, the Pack had been without a leader. So they answered his call. They came to the Council Rock and saw Shere Khan's striped coat on the rock. They saw and heard Mowgli sing and dance upon the tiger's hide.

I, Mowgli, am singing. Let the Jungle listen.
I dance on the hide of Shere Khan,
but my heart is very heavy.
My mouth is cut with the stones from the village,
but my heart is very light,
because I have come back to the Jungle.
These two things fight together in me,
like the snakes fight in the spring.
The water comes out of my eyes;
yet I laugh while it falls. Why?
I am two Mowglis, but the hide of Shere Khan
is under my feet.
Look—look well, O Wolves!
Ahae! My heart is heavy with the things
that I do not understand.

"Look well, O Wolves. Have I kept my word?" said Mowgli.

All the wolves bayed, "Yes!"

One tattered wolf howled, "Lead us again, O Akela. Lead us again, O Man-cub, for we are not free when we have no laws. We want to be the Free People once more."

"Nay," purred Bagheera. "You wanted your freedom, and now it is yours, O Wolves."

"Man Pack and Wolf Pack have cast me out," said Mowgli. "Now I will hunt alone in the Jungle."

"And we will hunt with you," said Mother Wolf's four cubs.

So Mowgli went away and hunted with the four cubs in the Jungle from that day on. But he was not always alone, because, years afterward, he became a man and married.

But that is a story for grownups.

The White Seal

CHARACTERS

KOTICK — the white fur seal of Novastoshnah who searches for a new seal home

SEA CATCH — Kotick's battle-scarred father, a huge gray fur seal

MATKAH — Kotick's soft, gentle-eyed mother

HOLLUSCHICKIE — young, unmarried male fur seals (the bachelors)

SEA PIG — the Porpoise

HUNTER and SON — the chief of the seal-hunters of the village and his son

SEA LION — a gruff resident of Sea Lion's Neck

SEA VITCH — a big, ugly walrus on Walrus Island

OLD SEAL — the dying seal who urges Kotick to continue his search

SEA COW — big, ugly, slow-moving seaweed-munchers who lead Kotick to a special place

CHAPTER ONE

Kotick

All these things happened several years ago at a place called Novastoshnah on the Island of St. Paul. Not many people come to Novastoshnah. The only people who come every year are the seals, by the thousands out of the cold gray sea. It is the finest spot for seals in all the world.

Sea Catch knew that. Every spring he swam straight for Novastoshnah to claim a good spot on the beach. Sea Catch was fifteen years old. He was a huge gray fur seal with a full mane and long, wicked dogteeth. When he lifted himself up on his front flippers he stood more than four feet tall, and he weighed nearly seven hundred pounds.

He had battle scars all over. Every spring he had to battle other males for a good place on the beach to raise a family. There were thousands of other seals hunting for the same thing. The whistling, bellowing, and roaring on the beach was frightful. From a little hill, you could look over miles of ground covered with fighting seals. They fought in the waves, they fought in the sand, and they fought on the smooth rocks.

Their wives came to the island in late spring. The younger males, who had no need to battle, went inland and played about on the sand dunes. They were called the holluschickie—the bachelors —and there were two hundred thousand of them.

Sea Catch's wife was Matkah, a soft, gentle-eyed seal. When she arrived in June, he said to her gruffly, "Late as usual. Where *have* you been?"

Matkah simply cooed, "How thoughtful of you! You've taken the old place again."

"Yes, but look at me!" said Sea Catch.

He was scratched and bleeding in twenty places. One eye was almost out, and his sides were torn.

"Oh, you men, you men!" Matkah said. She fanned herself with her back flipper. "Why can't you choose your places without fighting for them?"

"Because our beach is so crowded," grunted Sea Catch. "I've met at least a hundred seals from another beach—all house hunting. Why can't people stay where they belong?"

"I think we would be happier at Otter Island instead of this crowded place," said Matkah.

"Bah! Only the holluschickie go to Otter Island. If we went there they would say we were afraid."

Sea Catch sunk his head into his fat shoulders and pretended to go to sleep. But all the time he was keeping a sharp lookout for a fight.

Matkah's baby was born not long after. His name was Kotick. He was all head and shoulders, with pale blue eyes, like all baby seals. But there was something about his coat that made his mother look at him very closely.

"Sea Catch," she said, "our baby is going to be white!"

"Empty clamshells and dry seaweed!" snorted Sea Catch. "There never has been such a thing in the world as a white seal."

"I can't help that," said Matkah. "There's going to be now."

And she sang the low, crooning seal song that all the mother seals sing to their babies:

THE WHITE SEAL

You mustn't swim till you're six weeks old,
Or your head will be sunk by your heels.
And summer gales and Killer Whales
Are bad for baby seals.

Are bad for baby seals, dear rat,
As bad as bad can be.
But splash and grow strong,
And you can't be wrong,
Child of the Open Sea!

Of course the little fellow did not understand the words at first. He paddled and scrambled about by his mother's side, and learned to scuffle out of the way when his father was fighting with another seal. Matkah went to the sea to get things to eat, and the baby was fed only once in two days—but then he ate all he could.

The first thing he did was to crawl inland, and there he met thousands of babies his own age. They played together like puppies. They went to sleep on the clean sand, and then played again in their wonderful playground.

When Matkah came back from her deep-sea fishing she went straight to the playground and called, just like a sheep calls for a lamb. She waited until she heard Kotick call back. Then she headed straight for him, lumbering right through all the baby seals. There were always a few hundred mothers hunting for their children through the playgrounds, and the babies were kept lively. But, as Matkah told Kotick: "As long as you don't lie in muddy water, or rub the hard sand into a cut or scratch, and as long as you never go swimming when there is a heavy sea, nothing will hurt you here."

Just like little children, little seals cannot swim. The first time Kotick went down to the sea, a wave carried him out. His big head sank and his little back flippers flew up into the air. The next wave tossed him back onto the shore. After that, he learned to lie in a beach pool and let the wash of the waves just cover him and lift him up while he paddled. He always kept his eye open for big waves that might hurt.

Kotick spent two weeks learning to use his flippers. He splashed in and out of the water, coughed and grunted, and crawled up the beach to take naps on the sand. Then he went back again, until at last he found that he truly belonged to the water. You can imagine the fun he had with his friends, ducking under the waves, or riding them all the way up onto the beach. Sometimes they played "I'm the King of the Castle" on the slippery, weedy rocks.

Now and then he saw a thin fin, like a big shark's fin, drifting along close to shore. He knew this was the Killer Whale, who eats young seals when he can get them. Kotick would head for the beach like an arrow, and the fin would slide away slowly in the water.

Late in October the seal families began to leave St. Paul for the deep sea. Only the holluschickie stayed behind to play anywhere they liked.

"Next year," said Matkah to Kotick, "you will be a holluschickie. But this year you must learn how to catch fish."

They set out together across the Pacific Ocean. Matkah showed Kotick how to sleep on his back with his flippers tucked down by his side and his little nose just out of the water. He also learned the "feel of the water." When Kotick felt his skin tingle all over, Matkah told him that this meant bad weather coming, and he must swim hard and get away.

"In a little time," she said, "you'll know where to swim to. But for now we'll follow Sea Pig, the Porpoise, for he is very wise."

A school of porpoises were ducking and racing through the water, and little Kotick followed them as fast as he could.

"How do you know where to go to?" he panted to the leader.

The leader rolled his white eye and ducked under. "My tail tingles, youngster," he said. "That means there's a storm behind me. Come along!"

Kotick learned many things. Matkah taught him to follow the fish along the undersea banks. He learned how to swim in and around the shipwrecks lying on the sand. He learned how to dance on the top of the waves when the lightning was racing all over the sky. He learned how to jump three or four feet out of the water like a dolphin. And he learned to never stop and look at a boat or a ship, especially a rowboat. At the end of six months, he had learned much about deep-sea fishing—and all that time he never set flipper on dry ground.

CHAPTER TWO

"It's Horrible"

One day, Kotick was lying half asleep in the warm water, bored and lazy. He remembered the good firm beaches of Novastoshnah seven thousand miles away. He thought of the games his friends played. He thought of the smell of the seaweed and the roars of the fighting seals. That very minute he turned north and began swimming. As he went, he met many other seals, all headed for the same place.

"Greeting, Kotick!" they said. "This year we are all holluschickie! We can dance the Fire Dance and play on the new grass. Hey—where did you get that coat?"

Kotick's fur was almost pure white now. He felt very proud of it, but he said nothing about it.

"Swim quickly!" called Kotick. "My bones ache for land."

And so they all came to the beaches where they had been born. They heard the old seals, their fathers, fighting in the rolling mist.

That night Kotick danced the Fire Dance with the yearling seals. In the summer, the colored lights in the sky reflected in the sea. As the seals jumped and splashed, the sea was full of fire.

Then they went inland to the holluschickie grounds. They rolled up and down in the new wild grass. They told stories of what they had done while they had been at sea. The older holluschickie romped down from the hill crying, "Out of the way, youngsters!"

"Hi, you yearling," cried one. "Where did you get that white coat?"

"I didn't get it," said Kotick, getting ready to wrestle him. "It grew."

Just then, a couple of black-haired men with red faces came from behind a sand dune. Kotick had never seen a man before. He coughed and lowered his head. The holluschickie just moved off a few yards and sat staring stupidly. One man was the chief of the seal-hunters on the island. The other was his son. They came from the little village a half a mile away. They had come to choose the seals they would herd off to their pens—to be turned into sealskin jackets later on.

"Ho!" said the son. "Look! A white seal!"

The older man began to mutter a prayer. "Don't touch him, son. There has never been a white seal since—since I was born. Perhaps it is a ghost."

"I'm not going near him."

"Don't look at him. Head off all the older seals. A hundred will do. Quick!"

The younger man charged a group of seals and herded them inland. Thousands of seals watched them, but then they went on playing. Kotick was the only one who asked questions. None of his friends could tell him anything, except that the men always came and drove seals in that way for a few months every year.

"I am going to follow," Kotick said, and he shuffled after them.

"The white seal is coming," cried the son. "That's the first time a seal has ever followed us!"

"Hush! Don't look behind you," said the father. "It *is* a ghost!"

The distance to the pens was only half a mile, but it took an hour to get there. Kotick followed, panting and wondering if he had reached the world's end. He could still hear the roar of the seals from far away on the beach.

What Kotick saw next was horrible. Many men with clubs came up to the seals. The men began to club the seals, killing them. Then the men took knives and skinned the dead seals. They threw the skins on the ground in a pile.

That was enough for Kotick. He turned and galloped (a seal can gallop very swiftly for a short time) back to the sea. At Sea Lion's Neck, where the great sea lions sit on the edge of the surf, he flung himself into the cool water, gasping for breath.

"What's this?" said a Sea Lion gruffly.

"They're killing all the holluschickie," said Kotick, "on *all* the beaches!"

The Sea Lion turned his head. "Nonsense!" he said. "Listen! Your friends are making as much noise as ever. You must have seen the men going off with one group. They've done that for thirty years."

"It's horrible," said Kotick.

"I suppose it *is* rather awful," said the Sea Lion. "But you seals come here year after year. So, of course the men know you'll be here. Unless you can find an island where no men ever come, you will always be herded away."

"Is there any such island?" asked Kotick.

"I haven't found it yet. But look here— suppose you go to Walrus Island and talk to Sea Vitch. He may know something. But it's a six-mile swim. If I were you, I'd take a nap first, little one."

Kotick thought this was good advice. He swam around to his own beach and slept for half an hour. Then he headed straight for the little, rocky Walrus Island, where the walruses herded by themselves.

He landed close to old Sea Vitch—a big, ugly, fat-necked, long-tusked walrus. Sea Vitch had no manners except when he was asleep—as he was then.

"Wake up!" barked Kotick, for the gulls were making a great noise.

"Hah! Ho! Hmph! What's that?" said Sea Vitch. He struck the next walrus a blow with his tusks, and the next struck the next, and so on till they were all awake.

"Hi! It's me," said Kotick, bobbing in the water.

"Well!" said Sea Vitch, and all the walruses stared at the young seal.

"Isn't there any place for seals to go where men don't ever come?" called Kotick.

"Go and find out," said Sea Vitch, shutting his eyes. "Run away. We're busy here."

Kotick made a jump in the air and shouted loudly, "Clam-eater! Clam-eater!" He knew that Sea Vitch was lazy and had never caught a fish in his life. He only dug for clams and seaweed.

Soon all the gulls and sea birds began screaming "Clam-eater! Clam-eater!"—for they liked to be rude. This made Sea Vitch roll from side to side, grunting and coughing.

"*Now* will you tell?" said Kotick.

"Go and ask Sea Cow," said Sea Vitch. "If he is living still, he'll be able to tell you."

"How will I know Sea Cow when I meet him?" said Kotick.

"He's the only thing in the sea uglier than Sea Vitch!" screamed a Gull. "Uglier, and with worse manners! *Stareek!*"

Kotick swam back to Novastoshnah to tell his friends what he had seen. But no one seemed to care. They told him that men had always taken the holluschickie—it was part of the day's work.

"If you do not like to see ugly things, you should not have followed," said one.

Kotick went and told his father.

"They only want the holluschickie," said old Sea Catch. "What you must do, is grow up and be a big seal like your father, and have a family on the beach. Then they will leave you alone."

Even Matkah, his gentle mother, said, "You will never be able to stop the killing. Go and play in the sea, Kotick."

And Kotick went off and danced the Fire Dance with a very heavy little heart.

CHAPTER THREE

The Island

That autumn, Kotick left the beach as soon as he could and set off alone. He was going to find Sea Cow, if there was such a person in the sea. And he was going to find a quiet island with good firm beaches for seals to live on, where men could not get at them. So he explored by himself from the North to the South Pacific. He swam as much as three hundred miles in a day and a night. He met with more adventures than can be told. He was almost caught by a Hammerhead Shark. He met all sorts of sea animals, but he never met Sea Cow. And he never found an island that was free of men.

He met an old albatross who told him about an island that was the very place for peace and quiet. When Kotick went down there, he found that the shore rocks were too jagged. Kotick went from island to island, but not one would have made a home for seals. So he went back to Novastoshnah to rest for the summer.

The holluschickie made fun of him and his grand dreams. But still he searched. Kotick spent five seasons exploring, resting each summer at Novastoshnah.

Everywhere he went, the People of the Sea told him the same things. Seals had come to those islands once upon a time, but men had killed them all off. Even when he swam thousands of miles out of the Pacific, he found a few scraggly seals on a rock, and they told him that men came there too.

That nearly broke his heart, and he headed back to his own beach. On his way north he rested on an island full of green trees. There he found an old, old seal who was dying. Kotick caught fish for him and told him all his sorrows.

"Now," said Kotick sadly, "I am going back to Novastoshnah. And if I am driven to the killing pens with the holluschickie, I don't care."

The Old Seal said, "Try once more. I am the last of my family. In the days when men killed us by the thousands, there was a story that someday a white seal would come out of the North. The white seal would lead the seal people to a quiet place. I am old, and I will never live to see that day, but others will. Try once more."

And Kotick curled up his mustache (it was a beauty) and said, "I am the only white seal that has ever been born. I am the only seal, black or white, who ever thought of looking for new islands."

This cheered him up. When he came back to Novastoshnah that summer, he was no longer a holluschickie. He was a full-grown seal with a curly white mane, as heavy, as big, and as fierce as his father. His mother begged him to marry and settle down.

"Give me another season," he said.

Now, there was another seal who thought she would put off marrying till the next year. Kotick danced the Fire Dance with her all down the beach the night before he set off on his last search.

This time he went westward. He followed the trail of a great school of fish. He chased them till he was tired, and then he curled himself up and went to sleep near the shore of an island. About midnight he turned over under water, opened his eyes slowly, and stretched. Then he jumped like a cat! He saw huge things nosing about in the shallow water, munching on the heavy seaweed.

"Who in the Deep Sea are these people?" Kotick said under his breath.

They were like no walrus, sea lion, seal, bear, whale, shark, fish, or squid that Kotick had ever seen before. They were twenty feet long. They had no hind flippers. They had a shovel-like tail that looked like wet leather. Their heads were the most foolish-looking things you ever saw. And they balanced on the ends of their tails in deep water when they weren't grazing.

"Ahem!" said Kotick. "Good sport, gentlemen?"

The big things bowed and waved their flippers. Then they began feeding again. They tucked seaweed between their big split lips and chumped slowly.

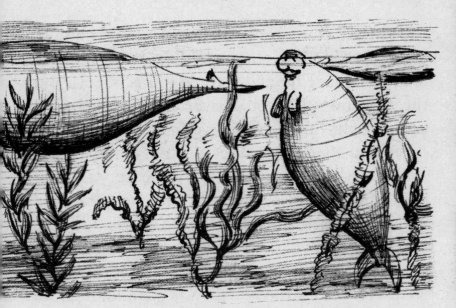

"Messy way to eat," said Kotick. They bowed again. "I would like to know your names."

The big lips moved and twitched. The glassy green eyes stared, but they did not speak.

"Well!" said Kotick. "You're the only people I've ever met uglier than Sea Vitch—and with worse manners."

Then he remembered what the Gull had screamed to him years before at Walrus Island: "He's the only thing in the sea uglier than Sea Vitch! Uglier, and with worse manners!"

Kotick tumbled backward in the water. He had found Sea Cow at last!

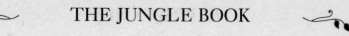

The sea cows went on schlooping and chump-ing in the weeds. Kotick asked them questions in every language he had learned in his travels. But the sea cows did not answer because Sea Cow cannot talk. But by waving a fore-flipper up and down and about, he makes a sort of clumsy code.

By daylight Kotick had become very tired of Sea Cow's slow swimming and stopping and bowing. Kotick followed them, saying, "These foolish people would have been killed long ago if they hadn't found some safe island. And what is good enough for the Sea Cow is good enough for the Seal. But I wish they'd hurry."

But they did not hurry. The herd never went more than forty or fifty miles a day. They swam slowly, stopped, ate, bowed, ate, and bowed some more.

One night they sank like stones through the shiny water—and began to swim quickly. Kotick followed. He never dreamed that Sea Cow could swim this quickly! They headed for a cliff by the shore and plunged into a dark hole deep under the water. It was a long, long swim. Kotick needed fresh air before he was out of the dark tunnel they led him through.

He rose into open water at the end and gasped, "Oh! It was a long dive, but it was worth it."

The sea cows were floating lazily along the edges of the finest beaches that Kotick had ever seen. There were long stretches of smooth rocks. There were playgrounds of hard sand. There were curling waves for seals to dance in, and long grass to roll in, and sand dunes to climb. Kotick knew by the feel of the water that no men had ever come there. And there was plenty of fish.

"It's like Novastoshnah, but ten times better," said Kotick. "Sea Cow must be wiser than I thought. If any place in the sea is safe, this is it."

He thought of the female seal back home. "I will explore this new country," he said, "and then I must get back to Novastoshnah."

He spent weeks exploring. Then he dived and went out through the tunnel and out into the open water. He looked back at the cliffs and could hardly believe that he had been under them.

He spent six days going home. When he pulled himself out onto land, the first person he met was the seal who had been waiting for him. She looked in his eyes and knew that he had found his island at last.

But the holluschickie, and Sea Catch, and all the other seals laughed at him when he told them what he had discovered. A young seal about his own age said, "You can't just come here and order us off like this. Remember, *we've* been fighting for our spots here. That's a thing *you* never did. You only went swimming about in the sea."

The other seals laughed at this, and the young seal began twisting his head from side to side, thinking himself to be fine indeed.

"I only want to show you a place where you will be safe," said Kotick. "All you understand is fighting. Will you come with me if I challenge you and win?" A green light came into his eye, for he was very angry at having to fight at all.

"Very good," said the young seal. "*If* you win, we'll come."

He had no time to change his mind, for Kotick's head was out and his teeth sunk in the blubber of the young seal's neck. Kotick knocked him over. Then he roared to the seals:

"I've done my best for you these five seasons past. I've found you the island where you'll be safe. But I see that you must have sense knocked into you. So, look out!"

Never in all seal fighting was there anything like Kotick's charge. He flung himself at the biggest seal he could find and bumped him and banged him till he grunted for mercy. Then he attacked the next. You see, Kotick had grown very strong from all his deep-sea swimming. His curly white mane stood up, and his eyes flamed, and his big dogteeth glistened. He was splendid to look at.

Old Sea Catch, his father, gave a roar and shouted, "He may be a fool, but he is the best fighter on the beaches! Don't tackle your father, my son! I'm with you!"

Kotick roared back in answer. His mother, Matkah, and the female seal he was to marry, looked on with admiration.

At night, Kotick climbed a bare rock and looked down on the wounded seals. "Now," he roared, "I've taught you your lesson. Who comes with me to the Sea Cow's tunnel? Answer, or I shall teach you again."

"We will come," said thousands of tired voices. "We will follow Kotick, the White Seal."

Then Kotick dropped his head and shut his eyes proudly.

A week later, Kotick led nearly ten thousand holluschickie and old seals north to the Sea Cow's tunnel. The seals that stayed behind called them fools. But next spring, there were more seals that left Novastoshnah, for they had heard how grand the new land was. Year after year, more seals left to go to the quiet, safe beaches where Kotick now sits all the summer through, getting bigger and fatter and stronger each year, while the holluschickie play around him, in that sea where no man comes.

Rikki-Tikki-Tavi

CHARACTERS

RIKKI-TIKKI-TAVI — the young mongoose who comes to live in the English family's home

TEDDY — a small boy who adopts Rikki-Tikki

MOTHER AND **FATHER** — Teddy's parents

DARZEE AND **HIS WIFE** — the tailorbirds who have a nest in a thorn bush in the garden

NAG — the black cobra, five feet long with a poisonous bite

NAGAINA — Nag's wicked wife who has laid her eggs in the melon bed

KARAIT — the small brown snake with a bite as dangerous as a cobra's

CHUCHUNDRA — the nervous muskrat who warns Rikki-tikki that Nag is near

CHAPTER ONE

Rikki-tikki Finds a Home

This is the story of the great war that Rikki-tikki-tavi fought single-handed, through the bathrooms of the big house. Darzee the Tailorbird helped him. Chuchundra the Muskrat warned him. But Rikki-tikki did the real fighting.

He was a mongoose. He was like a little cat in his fur and his tail, but quite like a weasel in his head and his habits. His eyes and the end of his restless nose were pink. He could scratch himself anywhere he pleased with any leg, front or back. He could fluff up his tail till it looked like a brush. And his war cry, as he scuttled through the long grass, was *Rikk-tikk-tikki-tikki-tchk!*

One day, a high summer flood washed him out of the underground den where he lived with his father and mother. The flood carried him, kicking and clucking, down a roadside ditch. He found a little wisp of grass floating there, and he clung to it. When the ground dried, there he lay all soggy in the hot sun on the middle of a garden path. A small boy was saying, "Here's a dead mongoose."

"Let's take him in and dry him," said his mother. "Perhaps he isn't really dead."

They took him into the house. A big man picked him up between his finger and thumb. He smiled and said, "Not dead. Just half drowned." So they wrapped him in cloth and warmed him over a little fire. He opened his eyes and sneezed.

"Now," said the big man (he was an Englishman who had just moved to India), "don't frighten him, and we'll see what he'll do."

It is hard to frighten a mongoose. A mongoose is eaten up from nose to tail with curiosity, and Rikki-tikki was a true mongoose. He perked up, ran all round the table, sat up, scratched himself, and jumped on the small boy's shoulder.

"Don't be frightened, Teddy," said his father. "That's his way of making friends."

"Oh! He's tickling under my chin," said Teddy.

Rikki-tikki snuffed at the boy's ear. Then he climbed down to the floor and rubbed his nose.

"Oh, my," said Teddy's mother, "and that's a wild creature! I suppose he's so tame because we've been kind to him."

"All mongooses are like that," said her husband. "If Teddy doesn't pick him up by the tail, or try to put him in a cage, he'll run in and out of the house all day long. Let's give him something to eat."

They gave him a little piece of meat. Rikki-tikki liked it very much. After he ate, he went out onto the porch and sat in the sunshine and fluffed up his fur so it would dry. Then he felt better.

"There are many things to find out about in this house," he said to himself. "I will stay."

He spent all that day roaming over the house. He almost drowned in the bathtub. He climbed up into the big man's lap at the writing table. He put his nose into the inkwell. At nightfall he ran to Teddy's room to watch how lamps were lighted. When Teddy went to bed, Rikki-tikki climbed up too. Teddy's mother and father came in to say goodnight. There was Rikki-tikki awake on the pillow.

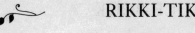

"I don't like that," said Teddy's mother. "He may bite the child."

"He'll do no such thing," said the father. "Teddy's safer with that little beast than with a watchdog. If a snake came into the room now—"

But Teddy's mother wouldn't think of anything so awful.

Early in the morning, Rikki-tikki came to breakfast riding on Teddy's shoulder. They gave him banana and boiled egg. He sat on all their laps one after the other. He enjoyed being a house-mongoose.

Then Rikki-tikki went out into the garden to see what was to be seen. It was a large garden with big bushes, lime and orange trees, and clumps of bamboo and high grass.

Rikki-tikki licked his lips. "This is a splendid hunting ground," he said. His tail grew brushy and he scuttled up and down the garden, snuffing.

He heard sad voices in a thorn bush. It was Darzee the Tailorbird and his wife. They had made a beautiful nest, but they sat there crying.

"What is the matter?" asked Rikki-tikki.

"One of our babies fell out of the nest yesterday," said Darzee, "and Nag ate him."

"Hm!" said Rikki-tikki. "That is very sad—but I am a stranger here. Who is Nag?"

Darzee and his wife hid in their nest and did not answer. From the thick grass there came a low hiss—a horrid cold sound that made Rikki-tikki jump back. Then inch by inch out of the grass rose up the head and wide hood of Nag, the big black cobra. He was five feet long from tongue to tail. He lifted himself and swayed back and forth, looking at Rikki-tikki with wicked eyes.

"Who is Nag?" said he. "*I* am Nag. Look, and be afraid!"

Rikki-tikki was afraid for a moment. But it is impossible for a mongoose to stay frightened for long. Rikki-tikki had never met a live cobra before, but his mother had fed him dead ones, and he knew it was a mongoose's job to fight and eat snakes. Nag knew that too—and *he* was afraid.

"Well," said Rikki-tikki, and his tail began to fluff up again, "do you think it is right for you to eat chicks from a nest?"

Nag was watching the grass behind Rikki-tikki. Nag knew that mongooses in the garden meant death sooner or later for him and his family. So he dropped his head a little and spoke quietly.

"Let us talk," he said. "*You* eat eggs. Why shouldn't *I* eat *birds*?"

"Behind you! Look behind you!" sang Darzee.

Rikki-tikki jumped high in the air just as something whizzed by under him. It was the head of Nagaina, Nag's wicked wife. She had crept up to make an end of him, but had missed. Rikki-tikki came down almost across her back. If he had been an old mongoose, he would have known to break her back with one hard bite. But he was afraid and he did not bite long enough. He jumped clear of her whisking tail.

"Wicked, wicked Darzee!" said Nag. The snake lashed up at the nest, but it was too high.

When a mongoose's eyes grow red, he is angry. Rikki-tikki's eyes were red! He sat back on his tail like a little kangaroo and looked all round him. But Nag and Nagaina had disappeared into the grass.

Rikki-tikki trotted off to the house and sat down to think. It was a serious matter for him. He was a young mongoose, and it pleased him to think that he had escaped a blow from behind. When Teddy came running down the path, Rikki-tikki was ready to be petted.

Just as Teddy was stooping, something wriggled a little in the dust. A tiny voice said:

"Be careful. I am Death!"

It was Karait, the small brown snake with a bite as dangerous as the cobra's.

Rikki-tikki's eyes grew red again. He danced up to Karait and swayed back and forth in the way mongooses do. It looks very funny, but it helps when avoiding the quick movements of a snake. Karait struck out. Rikki jumped sideways. The little snake's head lashed once more, and Rikki-tikki sprang over the wiggling body.

Teddy shouted, "Oh, look here! Our mongoose is killing a snake!" Teddy's mother screamed. His father ran out with a stick. Karait snapped, and Rikki-tikki jumped onto the snake's back. He bit the snake near its head, and the snake lay still.

Teddy's father began to beat the dead Karait. *What is the use of that?* thought Rikki-tikki. *I have settled it all.*

And then Teddy's mother picked Rikki-tikki up and hugged him. Teddy's father said that he was sent from heaven. Teddy looked on with big scared eyes. Rikki-tikki was amused at all the fuss, which, of course, he did not understand.

That night at dinner, he walked all over the table, but he did not stuff himself. He wanted to stay ready to fight Nag and Nagaina. Sometimes he gave his long war cry: *Rikk-tikk-tikki-tikki-tchk!*

Teddy carried him off to bed and tucked him under his chin. But as soon as Teddy was asleep, Rikki-tikki went off for his nightly walk around the house. In the dark he met Chuchundra the Muskrat creeping around by the wall.

"Don't kill me," said Chuchundra quietly. "Rikki-tikki, don't kill me!"

"Do you think a snake-killer kills muskrats?" laughed Rikki-tikki.

"Hush! Nag is everywhere. Can't you *hear*, Rikki-tikki?"

Rikki-tikki listened.

Scratch-scratch-scratch-scratch.

"That's Nag or Nagaina," Rikki-tikki said, "crawling into a bathroom drain!"

He scurried to Teddy's bathroom. Nothing there. In the mother's bathroom, he put his little ear to the drain that led to the outside. He heard Nag and Nagaina whispering in the moonlight.

"When the people are gone," said Nagaina, "*he* will have to go away, and then the garden will be ours again. Go in quietly, husband. Bite the big man first. Then come out and tell me, and we will hunt for Rikki-tikki together."

"But are you sure we should kill the people?" said Nag.

"Ssss! With no people, there will be no more mongoose. As long as the house is empty, we are king and queen of the garden. And remember— when our eggs in the melon bed hatch tomorrow, our children will need room and quiet."

"I had not thought of that," said Nag. "I will go do the killings and return with no noise."

Rikki-tikki tingled with rage. He saw Nag's head come through the drain. His five feet of cold body followed it. Rikki-tikki was frightened. Nag coiled up, raised his head, and looked into the dark bathroom. Rikki could see his eyes glitter.

If I kill him here, thought Rikki-tikki, *Nagaina will know. And I do not want to fight him on the open floor. What am I to do?*

Rikki-tikki heard Nag drinking from a big water jar. "That is good," said the snake. "Now, when Karait was killed, the big man had a stick. When he comes in for his bath in the morning he will not have a stick. I will wait here till he comes. Nagaina—do you hear me?—I will wait here in the cool till daytime."

There was no answer. Nagaina had left. Nag coiled himself down at the bottom of the water jar. Rikki-tikki stayed still as death. After an hour he began to move, little by little, toward the jar. Nag was asleep. Rikki-tikki looked at his big back. *If I don't break his back at the first jump,* thought Rikki, *he can still fight. And if he fights—oh, Rikki!* A bite near the tail would only make Nag wild.

It must be the head. The head above the hood. And, when I am there, I must not let go.

Then he jumped. Nag's head was lying a little clear of the water jar—and Rikki's teeth bit down!

The snake sprang up and whipped his body, shaking the mongoose like a rat, up and down, and around in great circles. Rikki's eyes were red and he held on! *Clang!* The snake's tail hit the tin dipper and the soap dish—*crack!*—against the side of the bath.

Rikki closed his jaws tighter and tighter. He was sure he would be banged to death. He was dizzy. He felt shaken to pieces. Suddenly—*bang!*—something went off like thunder just behind him. A hot, red fire burned his fur. The big man had fired a shotgun into Nag.

Rikki-tikki held on with his eyes shut, for now he was quite sure he was dead. But the snake's head did not move. Rikki loosened his bite.

The big man picked Rikki up and called, "It's the mongoose again, Alice. The little chap has saved *our* lives now."

Teddy's mother came in with a very white face and saw what was left of Nag.

Then Rikki-tikki dragged himself to Teddy's bedroom and snuggled under the boy's chin.

CHAPTER TWO

Rikki-Tikki the Brave

In the morning, Rikki-tikki was very stiff but quite pleased with himself. "Now I have Nagaina to deal with," he said. "She will be worse than five Nags. And who knows when her eggs will hatch! Goodness! I must go and see Darzee."

Rikki-tikki ran to the thorn bush. Darzee was singing a song at the top of his voice. The news of Nag's death was all over the garden.

"*Rikk-tck!*" said Rikki. "Is this the time to sing?"

"Nag is dead—is dead—is dead!" sang Darzee. "The brave Rikki-tikki caught him by the head. The big man brought the bang-stick, and Nag fell in two pieces! He will never eat my babies again."

"All that's true—but where's Nagaina?" said Rikki-tikki, looking carefully around.

"Oh, let us sing about the great, the red-eyed Rikki-tikki!" sang Darzee.

"Stop singing, Darzee!" said Rikki. "Where is Nagaina?"

"She is away at the stables, crying for Nag. Ah! Great is Rikki-tikki with the white teeth!"

"Never mind my white teeth! Where does she keep her eggs?"

"In the melon bed, near the wall. She hid them there weeks ago. Rikki-tikki, surely you are not going to eat her eggs!"

"Not eat exactly, no. Darzee, fly off to the stables and pretend that your wing is broken. Let Nagaina chase you to this bush. I must get to the melon bed, and if I went there now she'd see me."

Darzee was a silly little fellow, but his wife had sense. She knew that cobra's eggs meant young cobras later on. So she flew off from the nest and left Darzee to keep the babies warm and sing his song about the death of Nag.

She fluttered in front of Nagaina and cried out, "Oh, my wing is broken!"

Nagaina lifted up her head and hissed.

"You! You are the one who warned Rikki-tikki when I would have killed him!" Nagaina moved toward the bird as it fluttered away.

Rikki-tikki heard them coming up the path. He raced for the melon patch near the wall. There he found twenty-five eggs hidden among the leaves and grass. He could see the baby cobras curled up inside the skin. He began to bite off the tops of the eggs as fast as he could.

"Rikki-tikki!" screamed Darzee's wife. "I led Nagaina toward the house. She has gone onto the porch! Oh, come quickly—she means to kill!"

Rikki-tikki raced from the melon bed, holding the last egg in his mouth. He scuttled up to the porch where Teddy and his mother and father were having breakfast. But they were not eating. They sat stone still, and their faces were white. Nagaina was coiled up next to Teddy's chair near his bare leg! She was swaying to and fro!

"Oh, foolish people who killed my Nag!" hissed Nagaina.

"Sit still, Teddy," whispered his father. "You mustn't move. Teddy, keep still."

Then Rikki-tikki came up and cried, "Look at your very last egg, Nagaina!"

The big snake spun around and saw the egg on the porch. "Ah-h! Give it to me," she said.

Rikki-tikki saw Teddy's father grab Teddy and drag him safely out of reach of Nagaina.

"Tricked! Tricked! *Rikk-tck-tck!*" chuckled Rikki. "The boy is safe, and it was I—I—I that caught Nag last night in the bathroom." He began to jump up and down. "I did it! *Rikki-tikki-tck-tck!* Come, Nagaina. Come and fight with me!"

Rikki-tikki's eyes were like hot coals. Nagaina flung out at him. Rikki-tikki jumped up and backward. Again and again and again she struck, and each time her head came with a whack on the porch. Then Rikki-tikki danced in a circle around her. Nagaina spun—and grabbed up the egg into her mouth. She flew like an arrow down the path, with Rikki-tikki behind her.

As he was running, Rikki-tikki heard Darzee still singing his foolish little song. But Darzee's wife was wiser. She flew down and flapped her wings about Nagaina's head and slowed her down. When the snake plunged into the hole where she and Nag used to live, Rikki's little white teeth were on her tail, and he went down with her. (Very few mongooses care to follow a cobra into its hole.)

Up in the nest, Darzee said sadly, "It is all over with Rikki-tikki! We must sing his death song. Valiant Rikki-tikki is dead! For Nagaina will surely kill him underground."

Just as Darzee began to sing a sad, sad song, a dusty, panting mongoose dragged himself out of the hole, licking his whiskers. Darzee stopped with a little shout. Rikki-tikki shook some of the dust out of his fur and sneezed. "It is all over," he said. "The snake will never come out again."

Rikki-tikki curled up in the grass and slept, for he had done a hard day's work. When he awoke, he said, "Now I will go back to the house. Darzee, tell everyone in the garden that Nagaina is dead."

The happy news set all the birds in the garden singing and the frogs croaking.

When Rikki got to the house, Teddy and Teddy's mother (she still looked very white) and Teddy's father came out and almost cried over him. That night they fed him all that he wished. And when Teddy's mother came in to say goodnight, here was Rikki curled under Teddy's chin.

"He saved our lives and Teddy's life," she said to her husband. "Just think—he saved all our lives."

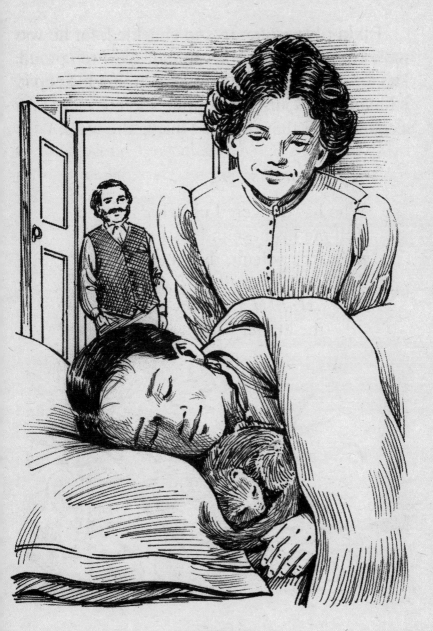

Rikki-tikki woke up and chuckled, for he was proud of himself. But he did not grow too proud. He kept that garden as a mongoose should keep it, with tooth and jump and spring and bite, till never a cobra dared show its head inside the walls.

Darzee's Song

Who has delivered us, who?
Tell me his nest and his name.
Rikki, the valiant, the true,
Tikki, with eyeballs of flame,
Rikk-tikki-tikki, the ivory-fanged,
    the hunter with eyeballs of flame!